I
Witness

SO-BUD-068

Million Dollar Winner

By Carol Gorman
Illustrated by Ed Koehler

CPH
SAINT LOUIS

To Ed

I
Witness
Series

The Taming of Roberta Parsley
Brian's Footsteps
Million Dollar Winner
The Rumor

Copyright © 1994 Carol Gorman
Published by Concordia Publishing House
3558 S. Jefferson Avenue, St. Louis, MO 63118-3968

Manufactured in the United States of America

Library of Congress Cataloging in Publication Data
Gorman, Carol.
    Million dollar winner/Carol Gorman
            cm.—(I witness; #3)
    Summary: When Adam's mom wins the lottery, Adam and his friend Ross discover they must forgive those who are jealous of them, just as Jesus forgave the people who hurt Him.
    ISBN 0-570-04630-0
    [1. Lotteries—Fiction. 2. Friendship—Fiction. 3. Christian life—Fiction. 4. Schools—Fiction] I. Title. II. Series: Gorman, Carol. I witness; #3
PZ7. G6693Mi 1994
[Fic]—dc20   93-36935

1 2 3 4 5 6 7 8 9 10   03 02 01 00 99 98 97   96   95   94

Contents

1

Adam's Surprise

If I live to be two hundred years old, I'll never forget that day. There were no hints that the good news was coming for Adam. It was a big surprise!

It was a typical fall morning. The sun was shining, and the leaves were falling off the trees. The kids, dressed in light jackets, piled into the school building as usual, talking and laughing.

I walked down the hall with my best friend, Adam Wheaton. Our whole fifth grade class was in the hall, along with the fourth and sixth graders, so we were getting jostled on all sides.

Adam was a pretty average guy: average looks, average in sports, average in school. You know what I mean. I was the same way. I suppose that's why we were best friends. We didn't try to compete with each other, we just had fun.

I was trying to get Adam to say he'd go to the circus with me that weekend. The Ringling Brothers were coming to town, and I couldn't wait to go.

"You've got to see the elephants!" I told him. We headed for the locker that we shared. "They're huge—much bigger than you think they'd be! The circus people ride around on them. The elephants even help put up the circus tents because they're so strong."

"Wow," Adam said.

"And wait till you see the trapeze artists! They can swing, turn somersaults in mid-air, and do lots of incredible things, and sometimes they don't even use a net under them!

"No net?" Adam said. "What if they fall?"

"They *don't* fall," I said.

Adam was looking at me, his eyes big. I could tell he really wanted to go.

"So let's plan on it!" I said. "Saturday."

"I really want to, Ross," Adam said. "But I can't. I spent my allowance already. I won't get any more money for two weeks."

"Can't you get an advance on your next allowance?" I asked him.

"No," Adam said. "Mom gave me an advance *last* week. That's what's already spent. Besides, she

6

doesn't pay me until *she* gets paid. And she doesn't get paid until the end of next week."

I knew that Adam and his mom didn't have much money. Mrs. Wheaton is divorced from Adam's dad. She works in a doctor's office and they live in a little apartment on the other side of the school. From what Adam had said in the past, I think they just barely have enough to pay their bills. Probably buying a ticket to the circus was a big deal to them.

I had to figure out some way that Adam could get to the circus with me!

"How about doing some work for somebody?" I asked. "You could earn the money for a ticket."

"Yeah," he said, suddenly looking happier. "That's a good idea. Maybe someone in the neighborhood needs their lawn raked or something."

"I'll help you," I said. "And you keep the money."

Adam grinned and socked me on the shoulder. "Thanks, buddy," he said.

We came around the corner and stopped at our locker. Adam turned to stare down the hall.

"What's going on?" Adam asked me.

There was a crowd of kids standing around somebody—or something. They all looked excited.

"Come on," I said. "Let's go see."

We hurried to the crowd and stretched tall to see over the heads.

"What's going on?" I asked Tiffany Gallagher, who was standing next to me.

"A party!" she said. "Hilary Ralston's having a birthday party. She's passing out invitations."

"Is everybody invited?" Adam asked.

Candy Miller turned to Adam. "Not *everyone*," she said. "Just the kids Hilary wants at her party."

Adam looked at me. "Do you think we'll get invited?" he said.

I shrugged. "I don't know."

"It's going to be at the country club," Candy said. "We're going to swim in the indoor pool. And the chef will be cooking pizzas for everybody. It's going to be really, really cool!"

"Sounds neat," Adam said.

Hilary had a handful of envelopes, and she was calling out names.

"Brit?" she said, looking around at the kids. "Is Brit here?"

"Yeah," Brit said, beaming. She reached out and took the envelope that Hilary handed her. "Thanks!"

"Juliet?" Hilary called out.

"Yeah," Juliet said. She took the envelope from Hilary, then turned to Tiffany. "Do we really want to go to this thing?" she whispered.

Tiffany grinned. "Sure," she said. "We don't have to love Hilary in order to have a good time at her party."

"Good point," Juliet said.

"Jake?" Hilary said.

Jake moved forward to get the prize.

I have to admit, I really wanted to go to Hilary's party. I'd never been inside the country club in my life, and I'd heard it was incredible. Everything is really expensive.

Besides, I just wanted to be invited. Only the "in" kids were getting invitations.

Adam and I stood there with the rest of the kids and watched while Hilary passed out the invitations.

"Tiffany Gallagher," she said. Tiff picked up her invitation.

"Abby Hart," Hilary said. Abby squealed and rushed forward.

"Jeff Heaton."

"Gabe Foster."

We waited through all the names, till every invitation had been passed out.

Then her hand was empty.

Adam and I looked at each other. We weren't invited.

The rest of the kids turned away, looking disappointed.

Brit, holding her white envelope, looked around at the others.

"You mean, you didn't invite *everyone?*" she said to Hilary.

"Of course not!" Hilary said. "My mother said I could only invite twenty people."

"You should have sent them through the mail," Brit said. "The rest of the kids feel bad."

Hilary shrugged. "That's not my problem," she said. She turned and walked away.

"Hilary's such a snob," Adam said.

"She sure is," I said. "Come on. Let's not think about Hilary's party. Let's think about the circus and how we're going to earn you the money to go."

We walked back to our locker, then went into the classroom. First we had reading, then social studies. In the middle of social studies, there was a tap on the classroom door.

We all looked up. Adam's mother opened the door and leaned inside.

"Mrs. Pettyjohn?" she said. "I'm sorry to interrupt, but could I talk to Adam for a minute?"

"Certainly," Mrs. Pettyjohn said pleasantly. "Adam, you're excused to see your mother."

Adam looked worried. He frowned and got up. He walked to the door and stopped. His mother motioned him into the hall, and he disappeared out the door.

I wondered if someone in their family had died or something. I said a quick little prayer, asking for everything to be okay.

It was funny, though. Mrs. Wheaton hadn't looked sad. In fact, she looked kind of happy and excited. But I couldn't think why she'd come to school in the middle of the morning if something bad hadn't happened.

Mrs. Pettyjohn went back to the social studies lesson. We were learning about the pioneers, and she told us about a video we were about to see. Then she put the tape into the VCR and turned it on.

Usually, I like videos. It's kind of nice to just sit back in the dark and watch the screen.

But this time, I had a hard time concentrating. I kept wondering what was going on with Adam and his mom. I turned to look at the door every few seconds, waiting for him to come back inside.

Finally, the door opened and I saw his silhouette in the doorway. He moved into the room and ducked under the beam of projected light, then sat down in his seat next to me.

In the dim light I could see his face. He was smiling.

I leaned over.

"What did your mom want?" I whispered.

He turned and gazed at me with a big grin on his face. "I'll tell you later," he said softly.

"*What?*" I insisted.

"Please pay attention to the program, boys," Mrs. Pettyjohn said.

I straightened up and turned back toward the TV. But I didn't hear a thing that was said. I just kept wondering what Adam was so happy about.

Finally, the tape was over, and Mrs. Pettyjohn said it was about time for a bathroom break. We all tromped out into the hall.

"So *now* are you going to tell me?" I asked Adam.

"I just can't believe it!" he said.

"Can't believe what?" I said.

"My mom came to tell me," Adam said, "that we're *millionaires!* We won the lottery!"

"*What?*"

Adam rolled his eyes and laughed. "Mom won a *million dollars!*" he said. "We're *rich!*"

2

The Invitation

*A*re *you kidding?"* I said.

"No!" Adam shrieked, laughing and throwing up his hands. "It's true! My mom won the *lottery!"*

Some of the kids standing near us turned around to look at Adam.

"Did you say your mom won the lottery?" Justin asked.

"Yeah," Adam said. "We won a million dollars! She didn't even know it until today when she heard there'd been a winner and she checked her ticket."

Stacy Wilson turned around from a group of girls. "Your mom won a million dollars?" she said. Her eyes looked as big as the silver dollars in my Uncle Bert's coin collection.

"Yeah," Adam said. "I just can't believe it!"

"Oh, wow!" Abby Hart cried. "I wish *my* mom would win the lottery! I'd buy, buy, buy!"

"What are you and your mom going to do with all that money?" I asked Adam.

Adam couldn't stop grinning. "I don't know," he said. "I can't think straight. This is so *awesome!*"

"I know one thing you can do with the money," I said.

"What?"

"You can go to the circus with me ," I said.

"Sure!" Adam said.

By now we were surrounded with kids. They all started talking at once, asking him questions.

"How'd you win the money, Adam?"

"Where did your mom buy the ticket? Maybe if *my* mom gets a ticket there, we'll win, too!"

"Is your mom going to give you half of her money?"

"Can you loan me ten bucks, pal? Ha, ha, ha!"

It was pretty wild. Adam had never gotten so much attention. My own parents never bought lottery tickets. Dad said it's like gambling. And he felt like God wanted him to use the abilities He'd given him to earn money. But I knew Dad and Mom would be glad for Adam. I stood there and watched him and felt really happy for him and his mom.

I thought about how many times I'd seen his mom look worried about not having enough money to get things for Adam after their bills were paid. I'd seen Adam look disappointed about not being able to buy tapes or CD's, or go to the movies or the high school football games that the other kids were going to because he didn't have the money.

Now that was over. Adam and his mom wouldn't have to worry about money ever again. They were rich! Could God have given them this money? I guess not. But God could sure bring them some good because of the money.

When it was time to go back into the classroom, everyone followed Adam inside.

"Mrs. Pettyjohn!" said Gabe Foster. "Did you hear the news about Adam?"

"What news?" asked Mrs. Pettyjohn.

"He's a millionaire!" about ten kids shouted at once.

"A millionaire!" exclaimed Mrs. Pettyjohn. "What do you mean?"

"His mom won the lottery!" called out Mike Heaton.

"Really?" she said, turning to Adam.

Adam grinned and nodded. "That's what my mom came to tell me."

Mrs. Pettyjohn beamed. "Well, what happy news, Adam! Congratulations to you and to your mother!"

"Thanks," Adam said. He looked at me and grinned some more.

Hilary stood up at her seat. This was the first she'd heard of our class's million dollar winner. Her mouth was hanging open so far, I could have tossed a golf ball down her throat.

"You're not kidding?" she said. "You really, *really* won a million dollars?"

"Yeah," Adam said. "Really."

"AAHHHHHH!" she groaned dramatically and sank back into her seat. "Why couldn't it have been *my* family? A *MILLION DOLLARS!* What I couldn't do with a million dollars!"

"Well, I think that's very exciting," said Mrs. Pettyjohn.

"Do you think if we all shake Adam's hand," Juliet asked, "his good luck will rub off on us?"

The kids laughed and two of the guys closest to Adam grabbed his hands and pumped them hard.

Another kid rubbed his hand on top of Adam's head. Then he held up his hand. "I won't wash it," he said, "until I go to the store with my mom and buy a lottery ticket!"

"I don't think it works that way," Mrs. Pettyjohn said, smiling.

"Well, he's the luckiest kid *I* know!" Juliet said.

"Adam and his mother are very fortunate, indeed," said Mrs. Pettyjohn. "Now, I know it's going to be hard to come down after all this excitement, but we've got schoolwork to do!"

We all groaned. Who could think about the pioneers at a time like this?

Mrs. Pettyjohn started talking about social studies again. I looked over at Adam. He sat, looking straight ahead, with his eyes unfocused. He had a little smile on his face.

I knew he wasn't thinking about school or Mrs. Pettyjohn or what we were going to do next in social studies. He was daydreaming. He was spending all that money in his mind.

I'd never seen him look happier.

I could hardly wait for lunch. Adam and I always sit together in the lunchroom at the table nearest the exit. I wanted to talk some more to Adam and find out what his plans were about spending the money.

I couldn't believe how long it took for lunchtime to come! The hands on the clock dragged so slowly I thought a couple of times it must have stopped. Once, I raised my hand and asked Mrs. Pettyjohn if the electricity had been knocked out.

"No, I don't think so, Ross," she said. She smiled a little. I think she knew that, as Adam's best friend, I wasn't concentrating too well on school stuff.

17

It seemed as if *days* had gone by, but finally it was time for lunch. I scrambled out of my seat and pounded Adam on the arm.

"Come on!" I said. "Let's hurry and get to the lunchroom."

"Oh, Adam!" a voice sang out. I knew who it was right away. I didn't even have to turn around.

Hilary Ralston. She walked up and planted herself right next to Adam. "Adam," she said in a very sweet, gooey voice, "I'd love it if you could come to my party next weekend."

Adam looked surprised. He glanced at me. I rolled my eyes.

"It's going to be at the country club," Hilary said. She smiled and swayed a little from side to side.

Just then Candy Miller and Stacy Wilson, her best friends, appeared from behind and stood on either side of Hilary.

"You've *got* to come, Adam!" Stacy said.

"It's going to be so *cool!*" Candy added.

"Well, I—" Adam looked over at me again.

I made a face, then shrugged.

"Say you'll come!" Hilary said. "My mom rented the pool, and we'll have it all to ourselves!"

"I'll come if Ross can come," Adam said, pointing at me with his chin.

18

"Oh." Hilary looked hard at me, then back at Adam. She seemed to be thinking about it.

"Hey, I thought your mom said you could only invite twenty people," Candy said.

"Shut up," Hilary said softly to Candy. "I'll take care of my mother." She turned back to us. "Okay," she said. "Ross can come too."

Adam grinned and looked at me.

"It's so great to be wanted," I said sarcastically.

Hilary ignored my comment. "Saturday. The country club. Two o'clock." She said all this looking right at Adam. I think she'd forgotten I was there.

"Okay," Adam said.

Hilary, Candy, and Stacy grinned. "All right! Super! This'll be great!" they said all at once.

They turned and walked away, talking excitedly. I heard Stacy say, "We'll have a *millionaire* at the party!"

"Only the best kids are invited," Hilary said, and they all laughed and walked out of the room.

"Looks like we're in, buddy," Adam said, slapping me on the shoulder. He started walking for the door with a swing in his step that I'd never seen before. "From here on in, things are going to be *different!* I'm *rich!*"

3

The TV Interview

Adam and I stopped off at my house after school to tell my mom the good news.

"Oh, Adam!" my mother cried. "What a *wonderful* blessing! I'll bet your mother is dancing on air!"

Mom and Dad both knew how little money the Wheatons had. I think my parents even loaned Adam's mother some money once so she could take Adam to the doctor.

"Yeah, she sure looked happy," Adam said. "I can't wait till she comes home from work."

"She probably can hardly wait to get home!" Mom said.

"Can I go over to Adam's place for a while?" I asked.

"Sure," Mom said. "But when Mrs. Wheaton gets home, it'll be time for you to leave. I'm sure that Adam and his mother have a lot to talk about."

"We have plans to make!" Adam said, grinning. "But Ross can stay for a while."

He threw an arm around my shoulder. "He's my best friend."

Adam and I rode our bikes over to his apartment. We wheeled the bikes into the building and up one flight of stairs. Adam fished his key out of his pocket and opened the door.

Inside, we leaned our bikes against the wall and plopped down on the living room couch.

The phone rang, and Adam ran to the kitchen to answer it.

"Hello?" he said. He listened a moment. "Yes, that's my mom." His eyes got big. "An interview? On *TV?* Yeah, Mom will be home about five-thirty. But you'd better call and talk to her first. Sometimes, she comes home pretty tired—"

Adam stopped. "Hello? Hello?"

He hung up.

"There will be a TV crew here at five-thirty," he said.

I grinned. "You guys are celebrities!"

Adam grinned back. "I hope Mom doesn't mind. I'd better call her."

He picked up the phone again and dialed. "Mom?" he said. "We just had a call from KRCQ-TV.

The guy said they'd be here at five-thirty to interview you about winning the lottery."

He listened. His face fell. "I don't remember his name," he said to his mother. "I'm sorry. Yeah. I'm sorry. I should have had them call you. Okay. Bye."

"What's the matter?" I asked.

"Mom said she doesn't want to give an interview today," Adam said. "She has a headache and she says she needs a perm before she goes on TV."

"But the TV crew is coming anyway?" I asked.

"She's going to call them and try to get them to come next week," he said. "But I have to straighten up the apartment, anyway, in case she can't convince them not to come."

"I'll help you," I said. "Where do we start?"

"There are dishes in the sink from breakfast," Adam said. "Will you wash them while I vacuum?"

"Sure," I said.

We spent the next forty-five minutes cleaning up the apartment. It looked really terrific when we were done.

"Your mom should be happy with how everything looks," I said, looking around the living room.

"Yeah," Adam said. "It looks great!"

There was a rap on the door.

I looked at my watch. "It's not five-thirty yet," I said.

"I bet they're early," Adam said. He went to the door and opened it.

Adam smiled, looking relieved. "Hi, Mr. Kolosik."

Mr. Kolosik, Adam's neighbor from across the hall, stood in the doorway. He wore a big smile on his face.

"Hello, Adam," he said. "Your mother home yet?"

"No, but she should be here pretty soon," Adam said.

"I had to come over and ask," he said. "Is the rumor true?"

"What rumor?" Adam said, as if he didn't know exactly what Mr. Kolosik was talking about.

"The lottery," Mr. Kolosik said. "Did your mother really win a million dollars?"

"Yeah," Adam said, grinning. "She really did."

"Aw, you lucky boy!" Mr. Kolosik said, ruffling Adam's hair. "Just think, I'm going to be living across the hall from a couple of *millionaires!*"

"Yeah, I guess so," Adam said. He looked at me, then back at Mr. Kolosik. "Well, Mr. Kolosik, a TV crew is coming over in a few minutes, and I told my mom—"

Mr. Kolosik held up a hand. "Don't say another word. I'll vamoose." He grinned and winked. "That means, I'll leave now."

23

"Thanks," Adam said. "I'll stop by later."

"Just think!" I said. "You'll be on TV tonight! Then the *whole town* will know about your win!"

"Yeah," Adam said. He walked to a mirror on the living room wall. "Think I look okay?"

I couldn't help smiling. "Like a TV star," I said.

Adam held his hands as if he were playing a guitar and started dancing around the apartment, singing a song I'd heard on the radio that morning. "Maybe I'll get discovered and be a rock star. Think I could make it?" he said.

"Sure," I said, "if you could play the guitar."

He jumped on the couch and strummed his invisible guitar. "Oh, y-e-a-h!" he sang. "And I love you t-o-o!"

A sharp rap on the door interrupted his act. He stopped short, then laughed, leaped off the couch and bounded for the door. He opened it a crack.

A guy and woman stood there. The woman held a TV camera over her shoulder, and the guy held a tall stand with a light on the top.

"Is this the Wheaton apartment?" the guy asked.

"Yeah, I'm Adam Wheaton." He opened the door wider and the two walked in.

"Adam," I whispered. "Does your mom want you to let people in when she is gone?"

24

"No," Adam shook his head, a little confused. "But I guess she knows they were coming."

"I'm Jeff Walker and this is Marcy Trott," the guy said. "We're from KRCQ. Your mom here?"

"Not yet," Adam frowned. "She should be here any minute."

"Okay, we'll wait," Jeff said.

"Sit down—" Adam started to say. But the two TV people had already sat on the couch.

"Let's talk to the kid first since the mother isn't here," Jeff said to Marcy.

"Right." Marcy picked up her camera again. "Where do you want him?"

Jeff looked around the room. "Let's emphasize how small this place is," he said. He got up and wandered around the apartment for a moment.

"How about at the kitchen table?" he said. "It's pretty cramped in there."

Marcy nodded and moved into the kitchen.

I was excited that Adam was about to be interviewed on TV, but I thought Jeff and Marcy should have talked to Adam instead of about him. I mean, he was standing right there in front of them!

Adam spoke up. "I think I should wait until my mom gets home," he said.

"Don't you want your friends to see you on TV?" Jeff asked him.

"Sure," Adam said. "But I'd rather wait until Mom gets home before I get interviewed."

"Come on in the kitchen," Jeff said to Adam.

Adam walked slowly into the kitchen with his hands slipped into his back pockets. He suddenly looked very self-conscious.

"Sit down at the kitchen table," Jeff directed.

Adam hesitated. "Please, just wait until Mom—"

"We're trying to get this on the six o'clock news," Jeff said. "We need to hurry. This won't hurt."

Adam looked at me as if he couldn't decide what to do.

"I don't want to make you guys late," he said. "But—"

"Great," Jeff said. "Then sit down. We just want to ask you a few questions. It'll only take a minute."

Adam thought a moment. "Well, I guess if it'll only take a minute."

He walked to the table and squeezed into the chair next to the wall. The room was so small, there was hardly enough room for the table, let alone a person sitting on the far side of it.

Jeff sat at the table across from Adam. "What's your name, kid?" he asked.

"Adam."

Jeff turned and nodded to Marcy who turned on the camera.

"Adam," Jeff said, looking at Adam and talking into his microphone, "how did you feel when you learned that you and your mom were the winners of *one million dollars?*" Jeff thrust the microphone in front of Adam's face.

Adam suddenly looked really scared. He reminded me of the way a deer looks on the road when it gets caught in a car's headlights. His face turned white, and he stared, wide-eyed at the camera. He swallowed hard.

"Uh, how did I feel?" he said.

Jeff nodded.

"Well, I felt—s-surprised," Adam stammered. "I mean, I didn't even know about the money until I found out. I mean, my mom bought the ticket. I wasn't even there."

Boy, Adam's my best friend, but I have to say, he sounded kind of dumb. He was so scared, he wasn't thinking straight.

"Where did your mom buy the ticket?" Jeff asked.

"I don't know," Adam said. "She isn't home yet."

"Well," Jeff said, "I couldn't help noticing that you and your mother live in a very small, cramped apartment. How do you think your lives will change now that you're millionaires?"

"Uh, I don't know," Adam said. "I suppose we'll buy—buy more stuff. I don't really know. Like I said, Mom isn't home yet."

Jeff nodded at Marcy and she turned off the camera. "When did you say your mom would be home?" he asked, frowning.

Adam glanced up at the clock on the kitchen wall. "She said she'd be here at five-thirty. That's right now. You guys were kind of early."

Just then, we heard the sound of a key in the apartment door.

"There she is!" Adam said, jumping up from the table. He looked relieved.

Mrs. Wheaton appeared at the door and looked around the apartment. She must have thought it was pretty-well picked up, because she nodded a little, looking satisfied.

"Mom, the people from the TV news show are here," Adam said.

Mrs. Wheaton's face fell, but when Jeff rounded the corner from the kitchen, she forced a smile to come to her face.

"Hello, Mrs. Wheaton," Jeff said. "I hope you don't mind us coming over."

"As a matter of fact," Mom said, smiling a little, "I tried to catch you at the station before you left. I'm really in no shape to be interviewed today. This has all happened so fast—"

"That's okay," Jeff said quickly. "We interviewed your son, so we'll still have something for the six o'clock news."

"You interviewed Adam?" Mrs. Wheaton said, surprised. She turned to Adam. "How did it go?"

Adam shrugged. "It was okay."

I was glad she hadn't asked *me* how it went. I'm not very good at lying, and I sure wouldn't have wanted to tell Mrs. Wheaton that Adam looked like a petrified deer. I figured she'd see it for herself on the evening news.

Mrs. Wheaton walked Jeff and Marcy to the door.

"My head is spinning," Mrs. Wheaton said to them. "I don't quite know what to do first."

"I'm sure you'll get used to the idea," Jeff said. "I could sure get used to being a millionaire."

"Me too," Marcy said.

Mrs. Wheaton opened the door and the two headed into the hall. Jeff stopped and turned back. "Oh, Mrs. Wheaton."

"Yes?"

"Are you going to keep your job?" Jeff asked.

"Why wouldn't I?" she said.

Jeff shrugged. "Just asking."

Mrs. Wheaton smiled and closed the door. She let out a breath. "I'm glad they're gone!"

"Why?" Adam said.

30

"I haven't had a moment to myself since my winning the lottery was announced," she said. "People called all day at the office. Friends, relatives, patients who know me, and mostly reporters. Whew! What a day! I'm exhausted."

I took the hint and said I'd better be going.

As I rode home on my bike, I started wondering again how God was helping Mrs. Wheaton. It was an incredible blessing of money for Adam and his mother. I knew that even if God didn't help Mrs. Wheaton buy the ticket, He sure wanted the best for her and Adam.

"Thank You, God," I whispered. "Adam and his mom are so happy!" Winning the lottery was a blessing, all right, but I could see that it had made their lives more—well, hassled, I guess.

Oh, well, I thought. I'd take all the hassles if I could win a million dollars! I didn't know then, though, that this was just the beginning. There were a lot more hassles to come!

4

A Shock at School

Hey, Adam! Saw you on TV last night!" called out a voice from the crowd. Adam grinned and nodded back. Adam and I were walking across the playground toward the school building. It was almost time for the first bell to ring.

"Adam! How does it feel to be a TV star?"

Adam grinned again and shrugged. "Good," he said.

"Man," I said, "you're really a celebrity! *Everybody* must have seen you on TV last night."

"Hi, Adam. Hi, Ross." We turned to see Juliet standing next to the building.

"Hi," we said. We walked over to her.

"It was neat seeing you on the tube last night, Adam," Juliet said.

"Thanks."

She shifted her weight over one hip and stared at Adam. "Does it feel different?" she asked.

"Does what feel different?" Adam asked.

"Being rich," Juliet said. "Do you *feel* different? I mean, I've always wondered if rich people think the same way that other people do."

"I don't think I've changed at all," Adam said.

"Really?" she said, studying him. "Well, I guess you don't *look* any different."

"I don't think I've changed," Adam said. "I still get out of bed at the same time, and I still like to eat English muffins for breakfast." He thought a moment. "And math is still my hardest subject."

"Oh," Juliet said.

"But then, I've only been rich for—" Adam looked at his watch and screwed up this face, thinking, "for only about twenty-two hours. Maybe I'll start changing later."

"Well," Juliet said, "keep me posted, okay?"

Adam leaned against the building and looked thoughtful. "You know, I really don't feel any different. I mean, I feel *happy*. I know my life is going to be different now—"

"How?" I asked him.

"Mom says she wants to move," Adam said.

My heart started beating fast. "Away from here?" I asked. I was suddenly afraid that my best friend would move far away and I'd never see him again.

"No," Adam said. "We'll still be in town. Mom wants to buy a house in the same school district."

Instant relief. "Great!" I said.

"And Mom says I can have a dog!" Adam said.

"*All right!*" I said. Adam had always wanted a dog. "What kind of dog do you think you'll get?"

"We'll have enough money to get a purebred, and that would be kind of fun," Adam said. He folded his arms across his chest. "But I think I'd like to go down to the pound and save a dog from being put to sleep."

"Yeah," I said. "That's how we got Bob."

Bob is our dog. He's sure not a purebred. Mom says he's all-American.

Just then the bell rang, and we walked to the school entrance. Standing there next to the door was a sixth grader, Mike Strand

"Hey, Wheaton," he called out to Adam.

"Yeah?"

"Saw you on TV last night," Mike said.

"Yeah, I think everybody saw it," Adam said. We walked over to Mike.

Mike laughed. "You really looked stupid." He pretended to be Adam on TV, staring straight ahead and looking terrified. "I didn't even know about the money until I found out." He laughed again. "That was the dumbest thing I ever heard. You looked like a scared rabbit."

34

Adam's face fell. He turned away from Mike, his cheeks pink. Some of the kids walking into the school stared at Adam. Some of them laughed at what Mike had said.

Adam pulled me a few steps away from the door. "Did I really look stupid on TV?" he asked.

He looked hurt, and I really felt sorry for him.

"No," I said. "Mike is just jealous!"

"You think so?"

"Sure!" I said. "You're a millionaire. Mike wishes he could have big bucks too. But *his* mother didn't win the lottery, so he's trying to make you feel bad."

"Well, I *was* awfully nervous when the TV guy was asking me questions," Adam said.

"Anybody would be nervous!" I said.

"You think other people thought I looked stupid?" he asked.

"Naw," I said. I threw my arm around his shoulder. "Come on, let's go inside."

All during the school day, kids came up to Adam to say they'd seen him on TV. I'm sure a lot of the kids wished they could have won the lottery, but most of them looked happy for Adam. Nobody else made nasty comments about how scared he had looked on TV. Adam relaxed and looked happy again. That is, he looked happy until we had gym class.

We were playing softball up on the baseball diamond. As I said earlier, Adam isn't the best athlete in the class. Neither am I. We're not bad, though; I'd say we're about average.

Since Adam's mother won the lottery, everybody seemed to notice Adam more, and gym class was no different.

Jeff Heaton and Justin Talbot were the captains. For the first time in his life, Adam was chosen first. He was on Jeff's team. You should have seen the look on Adam's face. He was so surprised. But I could tell he was happy too.

Mr. Winegardner, our gym teacher, made a little *huffing* noise. I looked up at him, and he was staring at Adam. He looked kind of mad.

The rest of the teams were chosen. I was the sixth-to-the-last person picked. I was on Justin's team.

The game started with my team at bat. Tiffany Gallagher was up first. She hit the ball. It flew close to Adam who was at third base.

He ran to the ball to scoop it up off the ground, but he was so excited, he wasn't careful, and he kicked the ball before he could reach down to get it. It rolled along the ground, and he lunged for it, but he kicked it *again!* By the time he finally picked up the ball and threw it at first base, Tiffany had been standing there for maybe five whole seconds.

Mr. Winegardner laughed loudly. The kids looked over at him, and he shook his head and continued laughing.

Adam didn't play much better the rest of the game. I think he was so embarrassed at how bad he was on the very first play of the game, he couldn't concentrate. He messed up almost every time he had to play.

I could tell Adam was miserable. He kept his head down and looked at the ground for most of the game. Every time he had to come in to play, he flubbed it.

After one of his flubs, Gabe Foster yelled, "Hey, millionaire, you're going to have to do better than that!"

Some of the kids laughed.

I was standing close to Mr. Winegardner, and I heard him say almost under his breath, "You tell 'im, Gabe."

I don't think Adam heard that comment from our gym teacher, but he *did* hear what Mr. Winegardner said after class.

The whole class was walking into the building right behind Mr. Winegardner. The sixth grade teacher, Mr. Fenchel, was walking down the hall, and Mr. Winegardner stopped to talk to him.

Just as Adam and I passed him, Mr. Winegardner said, "If that Wheaton kid thinks his mother's million dollars is going to get him special treatment in my class, he's got another thing coming! I'll show him that money doesn't buy success in *my* class!"

Adam's head whipped around in surprise to look at Mr. Winegardner. The teacher didn't look at him. Adam turned back. His head sank and his shoulders drooped.

Almost everyone had heard Mr. Winegardner. I think he had *wanted* everyone to hear. The kids all looked at Adam. He slouched as low as he could.

We all kept walking toward our classroom. I put a hand on Adam's shoulder and whispered, "He's just jealous, Adam."

Adam nodded but didn't say anything. I couldn't think what to say. I'd always thought teachers were supposed to show *us* how to act.

We walked in silence back to class.

5

Hilary's Party

Ready to go?" I asked Adam.

It was Friday night and time for Hilary's party.
Dad waited outside in the car while I ran up to
Adam's apartment to get him.

He looked pretty excited about the party. He
was wearing a new pair of blue jeans and a new red
polo shirt that I'd never seen before.

Adam and I hadn't talked much about what
Mr. Winegardner had said after gym class the other
day. To tell you the truth, I couldn't believe a *teacher*
would say something that mean. Teachers are usually nice and they seem to really care about kids.
You never think that a teacher could be jealous or
mean.

My mom says that when people say nasty
things, it usually means that they are unhappy for
some reason, and that we should forgive them and
pray for them.

I know Mom was right, but I was too mad at Mr. Winegardner to forgive him *or* to pray for him. He shouldn't have said such a rotten thing about Adam. Adam didn't deserve it. Adam hadn't tried to get special treatment at all! And he couldn't help it that he was chosen to a team first. And he couldn't help it that he was nervous and didn't play very well. Mr. Winegardner was a mean, jealous man, that's all there was to it.

"Hi, Ross," Mrs. Wheaton said, coming out of the kitchen.

"Hi, Mrs. Wheaton," I said.

The telephone rang. Mrs. Wheaton walked to the phone and answered it.

"Hello?"

"Yes, this is Susan Wheaton," Adam's mother said into the receiver.

I nudged Adam. "Don't forget your swimming suit," I said.

"Got it right here," Adam said, lifting a white cloth bag.

"Did you get Hilary a birthday present?" I asked Adam.

"Sure!" he said. He pointed to a pink-and-green wrapped package on the couch. "It's a CD."

"Good idea," I said.

"What did you get her?" Adam asked me.

"A gift certificate to the Dairy Queen," I said.

"That's good too," he said.

"No, I don't need insurance," Mrs. Wheaton said on the phone. She rolled her eyes at Adam. "Well, if I decide that I need more insurance, I'll let you know."

Adam made a face. "You can't believe the people calling us!" he said. "Everybody wants us to buy something or give to their charity."

"Because of your lottery win?" I asked.

"They don't say so," Adam said. "But we've gotten twice as many calls since we won."

"No, you may not come over," Mrs. Wheaton said firmly into the phone. "I said I'd call you if I decide I need more insurance. Yes, I know I'll have more money now, and yes, I already have life insurance that will go to my son."

"Hang up, Mom," Adam said, frowning. "Don't let him bug you."

Mrs. Wheaton nodded to Adam. "That's all I have to say," she said. "Thank you anyway."

She hung up the phone.

"I wish they'd quit pestering us!" she said. "I think we should change our number. We'll get an unlisted one."

"Give *me* the number, though," I said.

Mrs. Wheaton laughed. "Ross, my dear," she said, "you'll be the first to get it!"

Adam and I said good-bye and hurried down to Dad's car.

"Sorry we took so long, Dad," I said after we piled into the car. "Mrs. Wheaton was getting hassled on the phone."

"Hassled?" Dad said. He pulled out of the parking space and into the street.

"Yeah," Adam said. "We've been getting calls day and night. Some people want to sell us something. Some want us to donate money. And some people just call in the middle of the night to bug us."

"That's too bad," my dad said. "Maybe you should change your number."

"We're going to," Adam said. "Someone even called my mom and said he was her distant cousin."

"What did he want?" I asked.

"A *loan*," Adam said. "A thousand dollars!"

"Wow!" I said.

"We don't even have the money yet!" Adam said. "It'll be next week before we get any of it."

"Won't you get *all* of it?" I asked. "Won't they send your mom a check for a million dollars?"

"That's what I'd thought too," Adam said. "But someone from the lottery office told my mom it'll come in smaller checks over the next twenty years."

"*Twenty years!*" I exclaimed.

"Yeah," Adam said. "We'll never see a million dollars at one time. And Mom says we'll have to pay a lot of the money to the government for taxes."

"But you'll still have more money than you did before," I said.

"Oh, yeah, sure," Adam said. "But we're not going to be rich or anything."

"Are you still going to buy a house?" I asked him.

"Yeah," Adam said. "The real estate people have been bugging us too. They all want us to buy a mansion or something. But even if we had lots of millions, we wouldn't buy a mansion. There are only *two* of us!"

My dad spoke up from the front seat. "Sounds as if your mom is being very sensible, Adam."

"Yeah," Adam said. He looked proud of her.

"Well, good for her," Dad said.

He turned a corner and the country club came into view. The huge building sat on top of a small hill and was surrounded by big old trees. Farther down, at the bottom of the hill was a golf course. The grass on the course was thick and green, and looked about as perfect as a lawn could look.

Tennis courts sat to one side. I had heard that on the other side of the main building were two swimming pools. There was a third pool inside. That's where we were going to be for the party.

"This is going to be fun!" Adam said.

"Yeah," I said. "Thanks for getting me invited, Adam."

"Sure," he said.

Dad turned to me, looking a little surprised, but he didn't say anything. He pulled up next to the stairs that led to the front door of the building.

"Have a good time, guys," he said.

"We will," I said. "Can you come back at four? That's when the party's over."

"Either Mom or I will be here," Dad said.

We said good-bye and climbed the stairs to the front door. It was heavy, but I heaved it open. Just inside was another door, so we pulled that one open too.

It opened onto a huge lobby with deep red carpet and heavy drapes at the far end. A grand piano sat silently near a side wall. There were several couches and wingback chairs sitting around and small tables with little lighted lamps on them.

"I wonder where everybody is," Adam whispered.

His whispering didn't surprise me. The room

44

was big and quiet. It was the kind of place that would make your mother say, "Lower your voice and speak quietly."

"I don't know," I whispered back.

An older man walked into the lobby from a back room. He looked kind of familiar, and then I realized it was Mr. Waterford. He goes to our church and is one of the richest people in town.

"Hi, Mr. Waterford," I said.

He looked over and broke into a smile. "Well, Ross," he called out. "How are you doing, and how are your parents?"

"Fine," I said. "We're here for a party. Do you know where it would be?"

He turned and gazed into a room off to the left. "I don't know for sure, but young people frequently meet in that side room."

"Thanks," I said.

Mr. Waterford smiled again. "Say hello to your parents for me."

"Sure," I said.

Mr. Waterford nodded to Adam, then walked out the front door.

"Man, I wish I had his money," I said to Adam. "Talk about millionaires!"

"Hey, there's Juliet!" said Adam.

Juliet stood just inside the room that Mr.

Waterford had pointed out. She looked over at us and grinned and motioned us to come over.

We hurried across the wide lobby and into the next room. Everybody was there for Hilary's party. The girls were all wearing skirts or special pants, and it was the first time I'd seen some of them look that dressed up. The guys looked pretty spiffy too. Most of us wore good jeans and nice shirts.

"Juliet," I said. "I can't believe you're wearing a dress!"

"Why?" she said.

"I've never seen you dressed up before, either," Adam said to Juliet. "You even wear pants to church!"

"Yeah," Juliet said. "Come to think of it, I guess this *is* unusual. I don't think I've worn a dress since my aunt's wedding last year."

This room looked a little like the lobby, only it was smaller. The ceiling was very high over our heads, there was a smaller piano next to the wall, and lots of windows along the side and back.

All the kids were milling around the room, talking excitedly and laughing. There wasn't any horsing around though, like shoving each other or running, because it was just the kind of place where you don't think of doing that kind of stuff.

"Oh, hello, Adam!" Hilary said, appearing suddenly at Adam's elbow. Her mother stood near her.

"I'm so glad you could come! Mother, this is Adam Wheaton, the boy whose mother won the lottery."

"Hello, Adam," Hilary's mother said. "Nice to meet you." She turned to me. "And what is your name, young man?"

"Ross Hunter," I said.

"Adam wanted him to come," Hilary said to her mother.

"Well, we're glad you both came," Mrs. Ralston said.

"Where do we put the presents?" Adam asked.

"Right here!" Hilary sang out. She pointed to a table along one wall. Presents wrapped in red, green, yellow, and blue paper were piled in the middle.

47

Adam and I put our presents on the table. Adam stood there grinning and stared at everything around him. Hilary and her mother left to greet some other kids who had just arrived.

"Maybe my mom will join the country club so we can come here anytime we want to," he said.

"That would be great," I said. "What do you think is out those windows?"

"Let's look," Adam said.

We walked over to the row of windows on the far wall.

"Wow!" he said.

In the ground below were two swimming pools sitting side-by-side. The water had been drained from them for the fall and winter, but you could tell they would have been great in the summer. A small cottage sat next to the pools. Huge trees grew over it and surrounded the whole pool area.

The lawn had recently been cut and raked. Only a few scattered leaves littered the grass.

"See?" I said. "Rich people have trees that rake up their own leaves."

"Right!" Adam said, rolling his eyes.

"Time for swimming!" Hilary called out above the crowd.

"Where's the pool?" Tiffany asked.

"Follow me," Hilary said.

48

"So much for dressing up," Juliet murmured.

We followed Hilary out of the room and into a narrow hall. She took us to a doorway half-way down the hall and walked through it.

There was the pool, sparkling blue and green under the overhead lights. There was one person there, the lifeguard.

"Great!" Adam exclaimed. "We have the pool to ourselves!"

"Of course!" Hilary said. "My parents rented it for the afternoon. Boys change in the dressing room to the left; girls are on the right."

In a few minutes we were all in the pool, splashing and jumping and diving. It was fantastic.

Everybody seemed to want to play with Adam. When we played water volleyball, Hilary chose him first. Stacy and Candy looked shocked and upset that they weren't picked first, but Hilary chose them next, so they calmed down right away.

Everyone passed the ball to Adam a lot, and he did a good job of batting it over the net. As a matter of fact, so did I. It was a great game.

After swimming, we got dressed again and tromped back into the room where we'd left the presents.

"Time to open my gifts!" Hilary announced.

She must have remembered which present Adam

brought because she grabbed his first and tore open the package.

Her face fell when she pulled out the CD.

"Just a CD?" she said.

"*Hilary!*" her mother exclaimed.

"But he's rich!" Hilary wailed.

"It was a lovely gift," Mrs. Ralston said. "Why don't you thank him properly."

Hilary turned an expressionless face at Adam. "Thanks for the CD, Adam," she said. She didn't exactly sound enthusiastic.

"Sure," Adam said. His cheeks and ears were bright red.

Hilary didn't really seem too excited about any of her presents. I don't know what she expected, but she did politely thank everybody for them.

Then we had pizza, cake, and ice cream in the dining room. We were served by two waitresses who called us *mister* and *miss,* and while we ate, they wandered around the tables, keeping our water glasses filled.

The kids were really impressed.

"Great service in this place," Juliet whispered to Hilary.

Hilary put her chin in her hand and flapped her eyelashes. "Oh, yes, the waitresses are such dears," she said.

Adam looked at me. *Dears?* He mouthed the

word, and I laughed out loud and a piece of cake flew out of my mouth and onto the white tablecloth. That cracked Adam up, and we laughed for the next five minutes.

And then it was time to go home.

We thanked Hilary and her mother and left. Most of the kids ran down the stairs to their parents' cars below. Dad's car wasn't there yet, so we leaned against the building to wait.

"That was pretty cool," Adam said.

"Yeah," I said.

"You really think my present was okay?" Adam said.

"Sure it was!" I said. "Hilary's a spoiled brat."

"Yeah," Adam said. "That's what I thought. The party was fun anyway, though."

"Yeah," I said.

"I'd like to join the country club sometime," Adam said. "It sure is a neat place."

"It sure is," I said.

"But promise me one thing," Adam said.

"What's that?" I asked.

"If Mom and I ever join the country club," Adam said, "punch me in the mouth if you ever hear me call one of the waitresses *dear*.'"

"You got it," I agreed.

Dad's car arrived then, and we hurried down the steps to meet him.

6

Popcorn, Anyone?

Practically the whole town came out to see the circus the next day. Adam and I could see how crowded it was when we were still a block away.

"Man! Look at all the people!" Adam said, walking next to me on the sidewalk. "Do you think we'll still be able to get tickets to the show under the Big Top?"

"Oh, sure," I said. "The tent is huge and holds thousands of people! We'll get in."

We walked closer and crossed the street.

"Look at the elephant!" Adam cried. "See that little guy riding him?"

"See? I told you!" I said.

Then I spotted a booth where a guy was selling stuff to eat.

"Have you ever eaten cotton candy?" I asked Adam.

"Nope."

"Then we've got to get some," I said. "You have some extra money?"

"Yeah," Adam said. "My mom gave me five dollars extra to spend."

"Great!" I said. It was great to hear him say he had "extra" money from his mom. That had never happened before! "Come on."

We ran over to the booth where a heavy guy with greased-back hair was leaning over the counter.

"Two cotton candies," I said.

"Three bucks," the guy said.

Adam and I each put in a dollar fifty, and the guy handed us some cotton candy on cardboard cones.

Adam stuck out his tongue and lapped off a piece of the white wispy candy.

"How do they make this stuff?" he asked after he had swallowed a couple of times. "It dissolves in your mouth!"

I laughed. "It's nothing but sugar with a lot of air whipped in."

Just then, Hilary, Stacy, Candy, and Abby walked by. They pointed to us and walked over.

"Hi, Adam. Hi, Ross," Abby said.

"Hi," we said.

I noticed that Hilary didn't say anything.

"You guys going to the show under the Big Top at one o'clock?" Abby asked.

"Yeah," I said.

"We are too," Abby said. "You guys want to sit with us?"

I looked at Adam. He nodded. "Okay," he said, but he didn't look too happy about it.

"Oh, good," Abby said, grinning at Adam. She looked over at Hilary, Stacy and Candy. Hilary was ignoring us, looking the other way. Stacy and Candy smiled. "Why don't you meet us just outside the entrance to the tent?" Abby said. "We'll wait for you."

"Okay," I said. "Five minutes to one?"

"Yeah," she said. "But get your tickets now while they still have them."

"Okay," I said. "Come on, Adam. Let's get the tickets."

Hilary looked bored and rolled her eyes. The girls walked away toward the lion cages.

"Hilary didn't seem too happy to see us," Adam said.

"So what?" I said. "She's a jerk."

I knew I really shouldn't call people names like that, but I couldn't think of any other way to describe Hilary. She was a *jerk* to Adam. She had only invited him to her party because he'd won the lottery, and she thought he'd buy her an expensive present.

I know Jesus wants us to love our enemies, but Hilary is a hard person to love! I was trying my best not to *hate* her!

"Hilary is so spoiled," Adam said.

"I know," I said. "Forget her and let's have some fun. Come on."

We walked to the booth and bought our tickets for the one o'clock show.

"I wish we weren't sitting with those girls," Adam said.

"Me too," I said.

Just then a clown clomped up to us, his big shoes flying out in front of him every time he took a step forward. He caught my eye and pointed to a big sign that hung around his neck: BE SURE TO BUY YOUR TICKETS TO THE BIG TOP! 1:00 p.m. SHOW.

He smiled then with a big dopey grin.

I couldn't help grinning back. "We got our tickets already," I said to him.

He winked and made an A-okay signal. We waved to him and moved on.

"Hey, Ross! Adam!" a voice called out.

It was Juliet Hollingsworth. She was with Tiffany and Brit. They ran over. Each of them was holding an ice-cream cone, and Juliet's ice cream was melting and running down her hand.

"Adam," Juliet said. "I was hoping you would be here. I wanted to tell you that we . . . " Juliet turned to Tiff and Brit and nodded to them. "We thought Hilary was awful to you at her party."

"She was so rude!" Tiffany agreed, nodding.

Adam looked embarrassed and shrugged. "Yeah, well, that's okay."

"She really owes you an apology," Brit added.

"She's a stinker," Juliet said. "She won't apologize. Hilary would *never* say she's sorry for *anything!*"

"Probably not," Brit said.

"Hey, are you guys going to the show under the Big Top?" Juliet asked us.

"Yeah," we said.

Juliet checked her watch. "It starts in twenty minutes. Want to sit with us?"

"Sure," I said.

"Yeah," Adam said.

"Let's go over there now," Tiffany said, "so we can get a good seat."

"Good idea," I said. We started off with the girls a few steps ahead of us.

It looked as if most of the people at the circus were thinking the same thing. They all seemed to be moving in the direction of the Big Top.

Adam nudged me. "Remember, we told Abby and those girls that we'd wait for them at five minutes to one."

"Oh, yeah," I said. "I forgot."

"Think we should 'forget' to wait for them?" Adam asked me.

It was really tempting. I wished we could just not show up at the entrance to the tent. But I knew that wouldn't be right. Abby would be disappointed, and she was pretty nice. I would have liked to avoid Hilary, but an agreement was an agreement.

"I wish we could forget it," I said to Adam. "But I think we should wait for them."

"Yeah, I guess," Adam said reluctantly.

"Um, Juliet?" I said. She and the girls turned around. "We told Abby and some others that we'd meet them in front of the tent just before one."

"Okay," she said. "We'll wait with you." She looked at Tiff and Brit. "Okay with you?"

"Sure," they said.

"Hey, there they are!" Adam said. "They got there early."

Up ahead, standing in front of the opening to the tent was Hilary, looking bored and standing with her arms folded; Stacy was twisting a strand of hair between her fingers. Candy was talking a mile a minute to Stacy, and Abby was listening to Candy's chatter.

Juliet stopped short. "You guys are sitting with *Hilary* and her friends?"

"Well," I said, "Abby asked us to sit with them."

"You're very nice to sit with Hilary, Adam," Brit said.

"Yeah, especially after how she treated you at her party!" Juliet said.

"She's such a jerk," added Tiffany.

"This'll be okay," Adam said, "with all of us there."

We trudged over to Hilary and Abby and the others.

"Hi," I said to them.

"Hi," Abby said. "Are you guys ready to go find seats?"

"Yeah," Adam said.

Hilary wouldn't look at either Adam or me. She looked bored and stared off into the distance.

"Let's go," Juliet said.

We walked into the tent. It was dark. Lights around the edges of the tent helped people find their seats.

"They'll turn the big lights on before the show starts." I'd said it to Adam, but Hilary turned around to gaze at me.

58

"Oh, really?" she said sarcastically. "I thought they'd make us sit in the dark."

The tent was very tall; it had to be tall so the trapeze artists could work. Bleacher seats were set up all around the edges of the tent, and in the middle were three huge rings where most of the acts would take place. The tent smelled of sawdust, animal droppings, and popcorn—a weird combination.

"Let's sit close to the center ring," Juliet suggested.

"Yeah," everyone agreed. That is, everyone except Hilary. She didn't say anything, but followed along, looking crabbier than usual. Stacy and Candy kept glancing at her, but they didn't say anything.

We chose some seats about half-way up the bleachers near the stairs on an aisle. Half of us sat down and the other half sat one seat above us. We spent the next twenty minutes watching people pour into the tent. They came in all sizes, colors, shapes, and ages—all of them looking eager to see the show under the Big Top.

I was excited for the show to start. I couldn't wait for Adam to see it, since he had never been to a circus before. I knew he'd love it.

The lights finally came up, spotlighting the center ring, and the ring leader began the show.

59

It was a great circus. We saw men and women performing tricks while standing up on horses that galloped around the tent. Once, while three horses ran perfectly together, side-by-side, the performers built a human pyramid, three layers tall. It was really incredible!

We saw performing elephants, a man who worked inside a cage with four lions, clowns, trapeze acts, and a fire-eater.

We had a terrific time, until *it* happened. It really was just a misunderstanding, but it practically wrecked the whole afternoon.

About halfway through the show, Adam nudged me. "You want some popcorn?" he asked.

"Yeah, that sounds good," I said.

Adam nodded and turned back to the row behind him. "You guys want some popcorn?" he asked.

The fire-eater was just doing his act then, and most of the kids didn't hear him.

"What?" Abby asked.

"Adam wants to know if you want popcorn," I said.

"Yeah!" Abby said. She turned to Hilary and Stacy and Candy. "Adam's buying popcorn," she said. "Do you guys want some?"

60

The girls' eyes got big. "Yeah!" they said. "Thanks, Adam!" Even Hilary smiled a little.

I should have known when they thanked Adam that they thought he was going to pay for *everybody's* popcorn. But I didn't get it until we had flagged down the guy selling popcorn, and he handed nine bags of popcorn down the two rows.

"That'll be eighteen bucks," he said.

I fished in my pocket for my share, and looked up. Everyone was looking at Adam.

He looked confused. Then he must have realized there had been a misunderstanding.

"Oh," he said. "Uh, I—I don't have—"

Brit spoke up first. "Oh, here's my share." She shoved the two dollars toward the man.

"I thought Adam was buying," Stacy whined.

"He's not?" asked Candy.

"What'd you expect?" Hilary said nastily. "I *told* you he's a cheapskate!"

"But you said—," Abby started to say to me.

"I didn't say that Adam was buying," I said. "Adam just wanted to know if you all wanted popcorn too."

Hilary exploded with a short laugh. "So the millionaire can't even buy some popcorn for his friends."

The guy selling the popcorn looked impatient. "Come on, come on," he said. "I need eighteen bucks. I only got six here."

"Give him your money, you guys," Hilary said. There was a note of triumph in her voice. She'd proven that Adam was cheap.

Adam sat and looked at his knees. The girls paid for their popcorn, and the man went away. Then Adam looked up. "If I'd brought that much money," Adam said, "I would've bought all the popcorn. I just didn't have that much with me."

"You don't have to say you're sorry, Adam," Brit said. "It was just a misunderstanding. No one should expect you to pay for everybody's popcorn."

"Of course not," Hilary said loudly. "No one would *ever* expect that rich Adam might be generous!"

"Adam, it's okay," Juliet said. "Really, it was no big deal."

I punched Adam's arm to let him know it was okay, but he sat there looking miserable for the rest of the show.

7

Adam's Idea

The popcorn episode at the circus really bothered Adam. Of course, it didn't help that Hilary, Stacy, and Candy were spreading the story all over school that Adam was a cheapskate.

They didn't tell the story the way it really happened either. This is what they said: Adam was acting like a big shot at the circus and bragging that he would buy popcorn for everyone. Then when the popcorn guy came over, and Adam realized how much he was going to have to pay, he said he didn't have the money.

"Adam-the-millionaire is a selfish cheapskate!" they said over and over.

Juliet and Brit and I tried to tell everyone what *really* happened. A lot of the kids believed us, I think. But there were an awful lot of kids who seemed to *want* to believe the story the way Hilary told it.

Even the kids who didn't believe it listened closely to Hilary's ranting and raving about how cheap Adam was. And no one but Juliet, Brit, and I defended Adam.

After morning recess, Adam and I walked into school and found a sign taped to Adam's locker.

ADAM WHEATON IS A SELFISH JERK! it read. There was another sign below it that said **ADAM WHEATON THINKS HE'S BETTER THAN EVERYBODY ELSE BECAUSE HIS MOM WON A MILLION DOLLARS!**

There were some kids standing around. They pretended they hadn't seen the signs, but all of them were watching Adam to see his reaction when he saw them.

I walked over to the signs, ripped them down, and tore them into about a thousand pieces. I turned to see Adam standing in the middle of the hall, staring at me. His face was bright red, and he looked miserable.

"You *know* who put up the sign!" I said to Adam. "It was Hilary."

"I know," he said. He spoke softly because everyone was staring at us.

"Why do you care what Hilary says?" I asked him. "She's a mean, rotten person, and—"

"Come here," he said quietly, and pulled me over to a far wall, away from the other kids.

"I don't want anyone to think I'm selfish," Adam said. "Or a jerk. Or a snob."

"You care what rotten Hilary says?" I asked.

He didn't answer for a second. Then he said, "I guess I do."

"Why?" I said.

"Well, for one thing," Adam said, "a lot of the kids believe what she's saying about me."

"Not the kids who know you," I said.

"Some of them believe her," Adam said. "Jeff Heaton and Gabe Foster haven't been very friendly today."

"Maybe they're just in bad moods. Maybe their moms yelled at them this morning," I said. "Just because they don't seem friendly doesn't mean they don't like you."

"They heard what Hilary was saying," Adam said. "I know they did."

"Then they're just jealous about your money!" I said. "They *want* to believe bad things about you because they're mad that *they* didn't win the lottery."

"Maybe," he said. He looked over his shoulder. "Everybody's staring at us."

"Don't pay any attention to them," I said.

"Do you want to know something?" Adam said.

"What?"

"Sometimes I wish Mom hadn't won the lottery," he said.

"*What!*" I exploded. "Are you kidding? You and your mom *need* that money!"

"But I don't want to be someone that everybody hates," Adam said. "I don't know what to do."

"You don't have to do anything," I said. "Just be yourself. Remember that before your mom won the lottery, you weren't best friends with everyone. You had some good friends, and the rest of the kids were just kids from the class."

"Yeah," Adam said.

"You didn't try to be everybody's friend," I said. "You weren't picked first for softball or volleyball, and you didn't really care."

"Yeah," Adam said again. "I know. But I didn't have *enemies*, either."

"You don't have enemies now," I said.

"Except for Hilary, Stacy, and Candy," he said. "And all the kids who believe what they're saying about me."

"But you shouldn't care!" I said.

I could see by the look on his face that he did care, a lot, and that nothing I said would matter.

"You'd care too," Adam said, "if a lot of people thought bad things about you."

I thought about that and decided he was probably right. I suppose if kids were talking about me the way they were talking about Adam, I'd be sad too. In fact, I know I would be.

I really hated Hilary for making Adam so sad. Adam should have been able to feel great because of all the money he was getting. But he didn't. He felt lousy.

It just wasn't fair that a few people could make a fantastic experience turn into a crummy one. And all because they were jealous and mean.

We walked into the fifth-grade classroom and sat down. Adam didn't talk much the rest of the day. Every time I looked at him, he was slumped in his seat, staring at his desk.

"I've decided what to do about what everybody is saying about me," Adam said on the way home.

"What?" I said.

We stopped at the corner and waited for traffic to let up before we crossed the street.

"I'm going to have a party," he said.

"A party?" I said. "How come?"

"If I have a party," Adam said, "and everybody comes and has a good time, they won't think

I'm a snob," he said. "I'll invite as many people as I can. It's not my birthday, so no one will think they have to bring presents. I'll call it something like a 'friendship' party. What do you think?"

I shrugged. "The name's okay, I guess. But I don't think you should do it."

"Why not?"

"Because," I said, "you *have* friends. You know you do. You don't need to have a party to prove anything to your real friends."

The traffic lightened up then, so we crossed the street.

"Well," Adam said, "I still think it might be a good idea. I'm going to ask my mom as soon as she gets home from work."

"Okay," I said. "When are you going to have this party, if she says it's okay?"

"This weekend," he said. "So I'll have to hurry and get the invitations in the mail."

"Yeah," I said, "whatever you do, don't hand them out at school the way Hilary did. That was so mean to the kids who weren't invited."

Adam grinned. "Like us."

I remembered then that on the day Hilary handed out the invitations, no one knew about Adam's million dollars. That was before he suddenly got popular.

"Right," I said. "See? And you weren't all that broken up because we weren't invited."

"No," Adam said. "But I kind of wished that I'd been invited. I really did."

"Yeah," I admitted. "I guess I did too. I wanted to see the inside of the country club."

"It was really neat," Adam said. "I loved that swimming pool."

As we turned the corner on Crescent Street, I said, "So who are you going to invite to your party?"

Adam reached into his pocket and pulled out a folded piece of notebook paper.

"I made a list," he said.

"You did that during school?" I said.

"Yeah," he said. "During science. I couldn't concentrate on school, anyway."

"Okay, so read me your list," I said.

He unfolded the paper and read, "You—"

"I like it so far," I said.

He laughed. "—Juliet, Brit, Tiffany, Jeff, Gabe, Justin, Paul, Abby, Stacy, Candy, Hilary—"

"What!" I said. "You're asking mean, rotten *Hilary*? Why, for crying out loud?"

"I'm trying to win over the kids who are saying bad things about me," Adam said. "How can I do that if I don't invite them?"

"Adam," I said, "I'm not trying to be mean, but this is a dumb idea."

"Why?"

"Hilary is your *enemy!*" I said. I knew last year's Sunday school teacher, Mrs. Jenkins, would have something to say about calling Hilary an enemy, but I didn't care. Hilary *was* Adam's enemy.

Adam didn't say anything for a minute as we walked along the street. I heard cars passing and our sneakers pad along the sidewalk, but I didn't hear a peep out of Adam.

Finally he spoke. "We're supposed to love our enemies," Adam said. "You know what Mrs. Jenkins always said about that."

"But why can't you love them from a distance?" I said. "Jesus didn't mean you have to invite them to your *parties!*"

"He *might* have meant that," Adam said.

I groaned. Part of me thought Adam wasn't talking sense, and part of me knew he was right. It was his party. So I decided to shut up. Adam should invite the kids he wanted. No matter how creepy they were.

Adam's Party

Adam's mom said he could have the party, so he sent out his invitations on Tuesday. The kids all got them on Wednesday when they got home from school.

Thursday was pretty weird.

The kids who already liked Adam were very nice, as usual, and excited about coming to the party. But the kids who had been nasty to him didn't know what to think.

Before school, Adam and I were talking together, leaning our shoulders up against the school in the sunshine.

I nudged Adam. "I think we're being watched," I said, looking over his shoulder.

Adam didn't turn around to look. "Who?" he asked.

"Hilary," I said. "And Stacy, Candy, and Abby."

"They're watching us?"

"And whispering," I said. "They're probably wondering why you invited them to your party. I mean, they must wonder why you'd want them after they treated you so crummy."

Adam smiled. "Maybe they've figured out that I've forgiven them."

I stood up straight and stared at Adam. "You've *forgiven* them?" I said. "Why would you want to do that?"

"I want them to like me," Adam said.

"Do you like *them?*" I asked.

"No," he said. "But I've forgiven them, anyway."

"I don't get it," I said.

"I figure I don't have to like them to forgive them," Adam said. "I hope they'll come to my party and realize that I'm not such a bad guy. Then maybe they'll stop spreading lies about me."

I almost said, "Dream on," but I stopped myself just in time.

"Uh-oh," I said. "Don't look now, but they're walking over here."

"Okay," he said.

I tried to look casual, as if I didn't see them coming. I stood there and kept my eyes on Adam and didn't look over his shoulder.

"So, uh, what are we going to do at your party?" I asked him. I tried to act casual.

"They still coming?" he whispered.

"Mmmm," I said.

He talked now in a louder voice. "Oh, well, we're going to play some games, eat some cake and ice cream, stuff like that," he said.

Now the girls were standing right next to us.

"Hi, Adam," Hilary said. I couldn't tell yet whether she was feeling friendly or nasty.

I have to give Adam credit; he's a good actor. He turned and looked surprised to see the girls.

"Oh, hi," he said.

"Are we supposed to bring presents to your party?" Hilary asked.

"No," said Adam. "It's not my birthday or anything."

Hilary glanced sideways at the girls, and Abby laughed.

"I won," Abby said triumphantly.

"What?" Adam said, looking back and forth between Abby and Hilary.

"I told Hilary you didn't want us to bring presents," Abby said. "But Hilary said you'd never have a party without expecting gifts.."

"Nope," Adam said. "Just bring yourselves."

"Okay," Abby said cheerfully. "See you."

74

"See you," Adam said.

Hilary didn't give Adam a second look. She turned and led the girls away.

I laughed. "Hilary couldn't decide whether to be nice or to be her usual crummy self."

"She thought I was having the party just to get lots of presents," Adam said.

"That's because *she* had a birthday party just to get the presents!" I said. "She thinks everybody else thinks the same way."

"Yeah," Adam said, smiling. "But I'll show her. By the time the party is over, all those kids will know I'm not a jerk, and they'll start acting nice to me."

"That would be terrific," I said to Adam.

I didn't know whether that was possible. But seeing the happy look on Adam's face, I hoped he was right.

On Friday night, I went to Adam's apartment early to see if I could help him get ready for the party.

"Everything's all done," Adam said. He was wearing his new pair of blue jeans and a new yellow long-sleeved T-shirt that I hadn't seen before.

"Not quite *everything* is done," his mom called out from the bedroom down the hall. "Will you boys pour the punch into the punch bowl?"

"Where is it?" Adam asked.

"In two gallon jugs in the refrigerator," Mrs. Wheaton said.

"Sure," Adam said.

Adam went to the fridge, pulled out one of the jugs, and handed it to me. Then he picked up the second, and we went to the punch bowl that sat on one end of the kitchen table.

"What's in this punch?" I asked him.

"I think there's some Hawaiian Punch," he said. "And some 7-Up. I don't know what else."

Mrs. Wheaton appeared, smoothing her dark hair with a hand. "As soon as the games are over," she said, "I'll add some ice to the bowl."

I looked over the table. There were forks laid out in a neat row along one side; a pile of napkins with printed pictures of balloons and flowers was stacked next to them; there were bowls of salted nuts and hard candy with little spoons sitting on top so we wouldn't touch any that we didn't put on our plates; and there was a big chocolate cake next to the punch bowl that said *ADAM AND HIS FRIENDS* in big red letters.

I wasn't surprised. Adam is a chocolate fiend. In the time it takes to say *Snickers*, he could scarf down three of them. The doorbell rang.

"Adam, would you get that?" his mother asked.

Adam grinned at me. "This is going to be fun," he said. "I've never had a party before."

He went to the door and opened it. It was Juliet, Tiffany, and Brit.

"Hi, guys," Juliet said, walking in.

"Hi," Adam said.

"Hi," Tiffany and Brit said at the same time.

"Don't close the door," Tiffany said. "There are about six other kids on their way up the stairs now."

In the next five minutes everyone arrived. At least I *thought* everyone arrived. Juliet, Brit, Tiff, Jeff, Paul, Justin, Gabe, Abby, Hilary, Stacy, and Candy were there, crowded into the small living room, yakking loudly at one another.

Then came another knock on the door. I jumped up and opened the door. My mouth dropped open. Standing there was that sixth grader, Mike Strand, who had made fun of how Adam had acted on TV.

I glanced over my shoulder at Adam. I wanted to say, "You didn't invite *Mike Strand,* did you?" But I knew that wasn't polite, so I just stood there with my mouth hanging open. "Oh, uh—" I stammered.

Adam saved me from having to say anything. He came up to the door.

"Hi, Mike," he said in a friendly voice.

"Hi," Mike said. He looked a little suspicious. Maybe he was wondering why he'd been invited to this party. He took a step into the apartment. He looked around the living room at the kids, all of them from our class, and scowled.

"Fifth graders!" he muttered, sounding disgusted.

"Sit down, Mike," Adam said.

Mike didn't move. He stood there with his fingers stuffed into his jeans pockets, looking self-conscious and ticked off that he was the only sixth grader there.

"Adam, will you come and help me?" his mother said, standing in the doorway to the kitchen.

"Sure," he said.

"I'll help too," I said.

Once we were in the kitchen, I grabbed Adam's arm. "Why did you invite Mike Strand?" I whispered. "He was so *mean* to you!"

Mrs. Wheaton turned from the sink to listen.

"I want him to like me," Adam said. "I thought if he had a good time here, he'd be nice to me."

I rolled my eyes and threw up my hands. "I can't believe you invited him!"

"We'd better get the games started if everyone is here," said Mrs. Wheaton.

"What are we playing?" I asked.

"I'll show you," Adam said, smiling.

78

Mrs. Wheaton handed Adam a stack of papers and a handful of pencils.

"Let's go," he said to me.

We went back into the living room where everyone was sitting like statues, crowded into the small room. They weren't laughing or talking or anything now. When Mike Strand walked in, the room had suddenly gotten quiet. Quiet as a tomb.

Everyone looked up when we walked in.

"The first game is a word scramble," Adam said.

"Great!" Brit said enthusiastically.

Mike Strand rolled his eyes and most of the guys groaned.

"This is just like school!" complained Gabe.

"Be a good sport, you guys," Juliet said.

Adam glanced around worriedly at the other guys, then passed out the papers. I got the last one.

"There are twelve words listed here with their letters in the wrong order," Adam said. "All you have to do is unscramble them, and the one who unscrambles the most words in three minutes, wins."

"This'll be hard," Abby said.

"All the words have to do with sports," Adam said.

"Can we start now?" Tiffany asked.

"Just a second," Adam said. He looked at his watch. "Ready. . . Set . . . *Go*."

We all bent over our papers and studied the scrambled words.

After a minute, Gabe groaned loudly with disgust.

After a minute and a half, Abby said, "This is *hard*."

After two minutes, Mike Strand wadded up his paper and threw it on the floor.

"This is *stupid*," he said. "I'm out of here."

He got up.

"Don't go, Mike!" Adam said. "The game's almost over, and then we'll do something else."

Mike opened the door and glanced back over his shoulder. "Are you kidding?" he said. "I don't know why I came to a stupid fifth-grade party anyway!" He left, slamming the door behind him.

Adam's face fell. He turned to the rest of the kids, then glanced at his watch. "Ten seconds left," he said.

"Who cares?" said Hilary.

"I only got two of the words unscrambled," said Brit.

"These were hard," said Tiffany.

"Time," said Adam.

"What was number eight?" asked Tiffany.

"I'll read all of them," Adam said. "Starting with number one, the words are basketball, goalie, umpire, bleachers, ticket, mascot, stadium, first base, cheerleaders, foul, strike, and puck."

"I only got two," Brit said again.

"I got three," said Justin.

"Isn't *first base* two words?" asked Tiffany.

"Hey, yeah!" said Candy. "It's written here as *one* word!"

"That's not fair!" said Hilary. "I could've gotten that one if you'd written it right."

"What was the last word?" asked Juliet. Adam looked at his list. "Puck," he said.

"Isn't it spelled *p-u-c-k?*" Juliet said.

"You spelled it like *puke!*" Paul said.

Everyone laughed, but it wasn't a good laugh. They were laughing at Adam for spelling the word wrong.

"I can't believe you're so stupid!" Hilary said. "No wonder we didn't get it. Only a dummy who couldn't spell would get that one right."

Adam's face got very red. "Uh, sorry," he said. "I should have looked it up in the dictionary."

"That's okay, Adam," Brit said. "It was an honest mistake."

Adam was too embarrassed even to smile at Brit.

"Did anyone get more than five of the words right?" he asked.

"I did," Juliet said.

"So did I," I said.

"Me too," said Paul.

"Did any of you get more than six?" Adam asked.

"I got six," Paul said.

"Me too," said Juliet.

"I got seven," I said.

"Okay," Adam said, smiling at me. "So Ross wins!"

Hilary made a loud *Hmm!* sound. "*Of course, Ross wins,*" she said. "He's your best friend!"

"Yeah," Stacy said. "He must have seen the words ahead of time."

"No, I didn't," I said. "Honest. I didn't cheat."

"Did you get *first base* right?" Hilary asked.

"Yeah," I said.

Her eyes narrowed. "Did you spell it as one word?"

"Yeah," I said. "I thought it *was* one word."

"Yeah, right!" Hilary said sarcastically.

"How about puck?" asked Stacy. "Did you write *puke?*"

"No," I said.

"Well, I still don't think it's fair," said Hilary. "Ross is Adam's best friend. He shouldn't be allowed to win."

"Of course, he should!" Brit protested. "He won fair and square!"

"That's okay," I said, shrugging. "I don't mind. Paul and Juliet can be the winners. They tied for second."

"That's better," Hilary said. She still sounded sour.

Adam turned redder than he was earlier. "But, uh, I don't have enough prizes for two winners," he said.

"Paul can have the prize," Juliet offered. "I don't care."

"You can have it," Paul said to Juliet.

"Well, make up your mind, Adam," Hilary said nastily. *"You're* the host!"

Adam looked miserable. This party wasn't going well at all!

"Maybe you could award one prize," suggested Brit, "and then give the second winner an extra piece of cake to take home."

"Great idea!" I said.

"Sure," said Juliet and Paul.

"Okay," Adam said.

Hilary rolled her eyes and *Hmm'ed* again.

The rest of the party wasn't any better. No one was in the mood for more games, but Adam didn't have anything better planned.

So we played Twister in the living room. That went pretty well until Gabe lost his balance and fell on Tiffany's wrist and hurt it. Adam's mother called her parents and said she would meet them at the hospital so Tiffany could have her wrist X-rayed.

"I guess we'd better have cake now," Adam whispered to me after his mom had left.

"Yeah," I agreed. "Good idea."

I slid a tray of ice cubes into the punch bowl while Adam cut the cake.

Brit walked into the kitchen. "Would you guys like some help?"

"No, thanks," Adam said. "Ross and I can handle it. Uh, sorry this party hasn't been a lot of fun."

"Hey, it's been a great party!" Brit said, but Adam and I both knew she was just being nice.

"You want to help me pass out the cake?" Adam asked her.

"Sure!" she said.

The three of us spent the next five minutes giving everyone punch and plates of cake with nuts and candy on the side.

"I hope Tiffany is okay," said Juliet when everybody was eating. She took a bite of cake.

"Yeah," said Hilary, raising her glass to take a sip of punch. She gave Gabe, who was sitting next

84

to her, a sly smile. "If Gabe weren't such a big ox, she'd be fine."

Gabe's cheeks turned red. "*Who's* a big ox?" he said, giving Hilary a shove.

Hilary's punch slopped out of her glass onto the carpet.

"Look what you made me do!" Hilary cried. Then she laughed and shoved Gabe back, spilling her punch again and knocking Gabe's cake plate out of his hand and onto the carpet.

Hilary stared at the red stain on the carpet. "Serves you right!" she said, laughing.

Adam stared at the stained carpet with a stricken look on his face.

"Oh, Adam, your carpet!" Brit cried. "Run and get some paper towels to soak up the punch. Does your mom have carpet cleaner around some-where?"

"In the kitchen closet," he said, hurrying to get the towels.

"Come on, you guys," Juliet said to Hilary and Gabe. "Cool it, will you?"

"You mean, like this?" Hilary grabbed a pillow next to her on the couch and threw it at Juliet. She missed and knocked over a plant on the window sill. It fell to the floor, spilling dirt in everywhere.

Stacy and Candy, sitting on the floor next to Juliet, laughed.

"No, Hilary," Juliet said angrily. "Knock it off, will you?" She got up to clean up the dirt. "Adam, where's your vacuum cleaner?" she called out.

Stacy, still giggling, reached over and grabbed Juliet's foot out from under her. Juliet caught herself on the edge of the coffee table.

"*I said knock it off!*" Juliet cried. She reached over to shove Stacy, but stopped herself just in time.

Stacy grabbed Juliet's arm and pulled her to the floor, where Candy jumped on her with a shriek. The three girls wrestled while Hilary laughed and shouted encouragement to Stacy.

"*Stop it, you guys!*" Brit cried out. She stood over them with a can of carpet cleaner in one hand and a large sponge in the other.

The other kids started shouting to the girls on the floor. Some were encouraging the wrestling match, others were yelling at them to stop.

A loud, shrill whistle sounded over all the noise in the room, and the girls stopped wrestling. The living room suddenly became quiet and everyone looked at where the sound had come from.

Adam stood in the kitchen doorway holding a metal whistle.

He spoke in a quiet, angry voice. "Everybody out," he said.

"You're throwing us out?" Hilary said.

"Out," Adam repeated. "Come on. Everyone. Get out. I've had enough."

The kids slowly stood up.

"This is the worst party I've ever been to," Hilary said, and flounced out the door.

"Sorry, Adam," Juliet murmured, heading for the door.

"Sorry, Adam," echoed Justin and Paul.

Stacy and Candy stifled giggles and left with the rest.

"I'll help you clean up," Brit offered quietly. She was the only one left.

"No," said Adam. "But thanks anyway." Adam and I stood alone in the living room after everyone was gone. It was a mess, with stains and dirt on the carpet and pillows scattered on the floor next to knocked-over chairs.

"What am I going to tell my mom?" he said.

"Let's get this place cleaned up," I said. "Maybe you won't have to say much."

He nodded and we got to work. Adam was quiet and I didn't talk either. What could I say on this horrible day?

I sneaked peeks at Adam and wondered if he could forgive Hilary and Stacy and Candy and Mike for ruining his party. I'd admired him for forgiving the girls before, and I knew Jesus forgave His most horrible enemies and wanted us to do the same. But just then, I couldn't imagine being able to forgive those kids.

Adam looked miserable.

Here he was, winner of a million dollars, and more unhappy than I'd ever seen him.

9

Mr. Waterford's Advice

My mom thought Adam might feel better if he did something fun, so we invited him to come with us to our church picnic the next day.

Adam and I hadn't told his mother about how the party had ended. We'd spent forty-five minutes cleaning up the living room, so it didn't look too bad.

We'd told her the party went fine. She seemed really happy to hear it. There didn't seem to be any reason to tell her the whole crummy story.

"Thanks for inviting me to come with you," Adam said.

"Sure," I said. "These picnics are always fun. So many of our friends go to our church."

"Yeah," Adam said. "It's like one huge family. Everyone at church has been really nice about the lottery win."

"Hey, there's Juliet and Tiffany," I said.

Juliet and Tiff were walking under a big oak. Tiff

had a cast on her wrist.

"Tiffany!" Adam yelled at her. "Is your wrist okay? Is it broken?"

She held up her cast and grinned. "I fractured it. Isn't it a beaut?"

"I'm sorry," Adam said, shaking his head. "My mom said later it was a dumb idea for us to play Twister in the apartment."

Tiffany laughed. "It wasn't your fault!" she said. "Or your mother's. Besides, I've never had a cast before. You should've seen all the attention I got at home last night!"

Just then, Mr. Waterford, the richest man in our church, walked up. He stood behind Juliet who didn't see him standing there.

"Adam," Juliet said, "we should be saying 'sorry' to *you*. At least, *I* should! We wrecked your living room and your party."

"It wasn't you," Adam said.

"I can't believe how mean those girls are," Juliet said. "They're so jealous that you and your mom won the lottery. They try to make you miserable every chance they get!"

"Excuse me," Mr. Waterford interrupted politely. "Ross, are your parents here today?"

"Hi, Mr. Waterford," I said. "Yeah, they're over near the big picnic table." I pointed at them.

90

"Thank you, sir," he said with a smile. He gazed over at Adam a moment. I guess he'd heard what Juliet had said about Adam winning the lottery. Then he walked off toward my parents.

"Anyway," Juliet said to Adam, "I'm sorry about your party."

Adam smiled and waved his hand. "Forget it," he said. "No big deal."

"Hey, some of the kids are starting up a softball game over on the diamond," Juliet said. "You guys want to play?"

"I'll be your cheerleader," said Tiffany. "I'm not supposed to play sports for awhile."

"Great," I said. "Let's go."

We tromped over to the diamond and played until we were called to come and eat. Then we stuffed ourselves on barbecued hamburgers, baked beans, potato chips, and fruit salad. Afterward, some of the adults in the church cranked the ice cream makers while we all stood around waiting.

Adam and I stood watching everything from a distance, sipping the last of our lemonade.

"Hello, boys," a voice said behind us.

It was Mr. Waterford. He smiled and nodded at Adam and me.

"Hi," I said. "Uh, Mr. Waterford, do you know Adam Wheaton?"

"I don't believe I've had the pleasure," he said, shaking Adam's hand.

"Hi," Adam said.

"I believe you're the young man whose mother won all that money in the lottery," Mr. Waterford said.

"Yes, sir," Adam said.

"Well, my hearty congratulations to you," said Mr. Waterford.

Adam smiled. "Thanks."

Mr. Waterford seemed to study Adam before he spoke. "Your friends must be very excited for you, I imagine."

"A lot of the kids are happy for me," Adam said. "Some of them who didn't pay much attention to me are acting like my best friends."

Mr. Waterford smiled. "Yes," he said, nodding. "And the rest?"

"Well," Adam said, with a quick glance at me, "some of the kids seem—well, kind of mad about our money. Even one of my teachers is being kind of mean."

Mr. Waterford stroked his chin thoughtfully. "Yes, I understand how that can happen. But remember, the friends who loved you before you won the money are still your good friends."

Adam nodded.

"You know, Adam," said Mr. Waterford, "there

will always be people who try and take advantage of you."

I thought about Hilary, who only invited Adam to her party because she hoped he would buy her an expensive present. Adam must have thought about her, too, because he looked over at me before he answered. "Yeah," he said to Mr. Waterford. "Already someone's done that."

"You don't have to let that bother you," Mr. Waterford said.

"I know," Adam said. "But I want people to like me."

"You can't make everyone like you, Adam," Mr. Waterford said. "Besides, it isn't *you* they don't like. It's that they wish they could have a million dollars too. They're envious. In fact, they're so filled with envy, they think if they can't have a million dollars, they don't want you to, either. My advice to you," said Mr. Waterford, "is to ask God to help you forgive them, and then turn your attention to your true friends, like Ross here."

"But if I don't pay attention to them, they'll say I'm stuck up," Adam said.

Mr. Waterford leveled his gaze on Adam. "*Are* you stuck up?"

"Well, no."

"Then you'll know that what they say isn't true,"

said Mr. Waterford. "Your friends know you. Your mother knows you, and God knows you. What does it matter what the others think?" He reached over and patted Adam's shoulder. "You're so special that God sent His only Son to die for you. He'll help you deal with other people. That's what's important." Mr Waterford smiled. "I just met you, and I'm impressed already."

"Thanks," Adam said.

"Listen to what I'm going to tell you," Mr. Waterford said. "Everyone has enemies. Even Jesus had enemies. It's not our job to change people's hearts. Only God can do that."

"Yeah, that's right," Adam said.

Mr. Waterford smiled again. "Don't worry about trying to please *everybody*. Ask Jesus to help you, and follow His example," he said. "You'll never go wrong if you do."

Mr. Waterford looked over at the activity around the ice-cream makers. "Well, boys, I think our dessert is ready."

"Yeah," Adam said. We turned to walk toward the picnic tables. "Mr. Waterford?"

The tall man turned to Adam.

"Thanks," Adam said.

"My pleasure, young man," Mr. Waterford said.

About a week after the church picnic, Adam and

I walked to the park for a game of catch. We played awhile, then sat on a green park bench.

"Remember when Mr. Waterford talked to me at the picnic?" Adam said.

"Yeah," I said.

"Well, I've been thinking about that," Adam said. "He makes sense. I guess everybody has people who don't like them."

"Sure," I said.

"Even the most perfect person who ever lived—Jesus—had enemies," Adam said.

"Right," I said.

"But Jesus forgave them, even while they were nailing Him to the cross," Adam said.

"Yeah."

"So I think I'll do the same thing," Adam said. "Mr. Winegardner hasn't been any nicer this week. And Hilary and Stacy and Candy still say bad things about me."

"They're jealous," I said.

"I know," Adam said. "But I can forgive them for the way they treat me. And now I know that it doesn't matter what those guys think or say about me because I know God says I'm okay. You know what I mean?"

I grinned at him. "Yeah," I said. "I know what you mean."

All of this happened over a year ago. Adam and

his mom moved into a small house near the park several months later. He got a really great dog at the pound and named him Snickers, because his coat has the colors of Adam's favorite candy bar. His mom is still working in the doctor's office and she's saving money for Adam to go to college. They seem really happy.

I think both Adam and I learned some important things about people when he and his mom won the lottery. There are people out there who don't want you to have good things. They aren't your true friends. But the best way to handle them is to ask God's help in forgiving them, and then to go on with your life.

Like Mr. Waterford said, God's love is what counts. He wants us to be happy. And one way He helps us be happy is to show us how to forgive the people we can't change. That's what Adam did. That's what I want to do. And I think that's just what God wants for us.